CHAPTER ONE

**My name is Howie. I was named after my father Howard, but it became too confusing to have two Howards, so I became Howie.
I am twenty-seven years old, and I work as a night manager in a supermarket.
This is my account.**

DAY ONE
FRIDAY

'The unseasonably hot weather has caught us all out. Not just our store but stores right across the region. Head Office is working round the clock to get the summer seasonal stock out to us. In the meantime, if we get customer enquiries, please remind them they can still purchase online and collect in store...'

My god, this is boring. I'm hot and uncomfortable. Being the night manager means most of this doesn't apply to me. I can't see our usual quota of taxi drivers, drunks, and whatever other poor sods coming into the store at night, asking why we don't have Bermuda shorts on offer yet, or why have we only got ten different sun creams instead of over bloody thirty of them.

'Onto other news...' the general manager drones on. 'The morning managers have reported a definite improvement on the readiness of the store for the daily trade. That, in my opinion, is down to the appointment of the new night manager...'

Shit, that's me. This is like being in school when the teacher stops and looks at you; then everyone else looks at you, and you get that fluttery, panicked feeling of missing the question.

'Er...' I sit up properly to see the other managers are all smiling at me. Apart from Paul, that is.

'We have seen an increase in trade during the hours of darkness too,' the general manager continues, 'and a drop in staff sickness and absence.' He peers down at a sheet of paper in front of him. 'Wastage has been reduced by over twenty percent and,' he looks up at me with that genial smile, 'unbelievably, we have seen an actual increase in sales of our promotional offers, which, ladies and gentlemen...' He casts his eyes around the room, '...Is unheard of for a twenty-four-seven store...'

I hate that fucking phrase. Twenty-four seven. It's just so, so...

'So, Howie, the floor is yours,' the general manager looks to me. 'Please impart how you have achieved this within three months of being appointed.'

Paul is glaring. Can't blame him, really. He was the night manager for twelve months and sat in these meetings every two weeks, moaning about how *"it was all so different*

THE UNDEAD. DAY ONE

SEASON ONE

RR HAYWOOD

THE UNDEAD
Day One
Season One

"Ready, Dave?"

at night" and *"you don't understand the pressures we're under."*

Different? Pressure? The only difference is that it's dark outside, and as for pressure, the bloody store hardly has any sodding customers cluttering the place up and making a mess.

'Ha!' I start off with a blurt of laughter, then inwardly curse at myself for doing it. *Yeah, great start, Howie, really great.* 'Um, well, we kind of, er... Just worked a bit harder?' I offer while feeling a blush creeping up my cheeks.

'Specifics, Howie,' the manager says, urging me to share my excellent managerial skills. 'Head Office is interested and wants to know what is being done differently.'

Ooh, that causes a ripple through the shark pool. These career-hungry bastards have just heard the words *Head Office* and *interested* in the same sentence. To have Head Office interested is either the precursor to a death sentence or something glittery and gold.

Paul isn't glaring now. The poor sod has dropped his head and looks beat, completely beat, like he's ready to start making a noose.

'Specifics,' I say slowly while rubbing my jaw to try and look all clever and serious. 'Well, er...staff absence is down because, er...'

What do I say? The night staff have been the night staff since time began. A collection of misfits and slightly odd folk, who, for many reasons, just don't like working in the day. Be that because they have a general hatred of humanity or an almost vampire-like existence, where the sight of the sun would burn them to death. No one knows. I can't tell the general manager it's down to the quick poker session we have during the lunch break either. That's really not allowed, like really not allowed.

'I think it's only too easy to see the staff simply as resources and not as humans with feelings and emotions.' *Oh shit, stop, Howie.* 'So in order to maximise the efficiency of the night staff, I simply make the working environment a nice place to be.' *Howie, stop, really stop now.* 'We all get on with each other and er...well, I may have bent the odd rule, not broken, I hasten to add.' Jesus, Tesco rules are carved in stone and carry a sentence of death by firing squad.

'What rules?' the general manager barks, losing his enthusiastic persona.

'Er, well, the spreading of breaks is the main one, really. I know during the day you have to make sure the break times are staggered, but on nights, we go down to a skeleton crew, which is rotated, and we take our breaks together, which helps build a feeling of camaraderie.'

'Right,' the general manager says slowly, as though he's just been told the secret to immortality, 'wastage?'

'Wastage?' I shift again. The reduction in wastage is down to getting barred from the poker game if you break anything. 'Er, just being like really careful...'

'The increase in promotional sales?' the general manager prompts. Everyone is staring at me now, apart from Paul almost weeping into his hands.

Yeah, the promotional sales. Whoever sells the most gets the first hand for free in the following nights poker game. 'Promotional sales? Well, that's just down to, er, an increase in promotional awareness and outlining the benefits of maximising sales, and how those benefits cascade down to everyone.'

'Good,' the general manager nods with interest, 'very good. A rising star in our midst, ladies and gentlemen, and someone to watch out for.' He beams round the room, happy again.

Cheers for that, I'll be testing my tea for poison now and watching out for trip wires next to the big waste crushing machines.

'Keep it up, Howie, and you'll be back on days before you know it,' he adds before finally turning his attention to the produce manager for an update on why sales of turnips have gone down. Thank fuck that's over.

I hate these meetings, but the good thing is that they earn me an extra night off. I'll stick around until my lot start at 9 p.m., then be off home for junk food, sofa, and maybe even a couple of beers.

Eventually, the meeting ends, and suddenly, I've got a whole bunch of new friends. Even the gorgeous cashier manager gives me a smile, which just makes me blush and walk into the back of a chair.

'Well done, Howie,' Steve, the home deliveries manager, pats me on the back.

'Head Office, eh?' someone else nods meaningfully at me. Duty managers, shift managers, staff managers, more managers than you can shake a stick at, but Tesco work to a formula, and as much as we all moan about corporate greed, they are bloody good at it.

The other problem with the big meeting is that all the managers are required to be at work at the same time, which translates to no spare office space, no free computers to work from, and not even a spare desk to sit at while the rest of them polish their name badges and slick their hair down.

Instead, I stroll about the store and smile at people while carrying some bits of paper. Always works, that does.

Five o'clock soon comes, sparking a mass exodus of office people running out the store to start doing whatever normal people do on Friday nights.

I get some office space and a computer and get my shit

together as the evening rolls on while listening to my small FM radio broken out of my drawer now the other tie-wearing bastards have all gone home.

By nine o'clock, I'm pretty much finished and stretching back, looking forward to my pizza and beer.

'*Reports from Reuters suggest the riot was sparked by one assailant biting into several members of the public within the shopping centre...*'

Did he just say biting? Bloody hell. I grab the radio and twist the volume knob up.

'*Details are still coming in, but we do know the area is being flooded with police in an effort to bring order...*'

'Evening, Howie.' Glancing up, I miss the rest of the report as Bert, the night shift security guard, walks into the office, prompting me to roll my sleeves up properly.

'Bert, how are you?'

'Smartness makes the man,' he smiles, giving me a smile that suggests he saw my scruffy half folded sleeves.

He's a grey-haired chap in his sixties, but Bert screams ex-army. His shoes gleam from being relentlessly bulled, and his trousers have razor sharp creases running down the front. His sleeves are either down and fastened properly or rolled up above the elbow with exact precision – something he likes to remind me about when he sees me looking scruffy.

'Meeting okay, was it?' he asks, taking a radio from the charging unit.

'Fine. Profits up, wastage and sickness down. They're very happy.'

'Didn't mention the poker games, then?'

'Funny that, no, I didn't,' I laugh as he adjusts his black tie. He holds the coveted position of CCTV controller, staying within the secure room to watch the millions of live feeds from the millions of cameras dotted about the store. Unless he's popping out to play poker, that is.

'Oh well, what they don't know won't hurt them. You're off tonight, aren't you?'

'Oh yes,' I grin, locking my fingers together behind my head as I stretch out. 'Pizza, beer, and my sofa.'

'Young man like you,' he tuts, 'should be out, finding yourself a nice woman. Or a bad one,' he adds with a wink.

'Yeah, one day... I'm still holding out for the cashier manager. She actually smiled at me today.'

'Did she now?' he chuckles. 'You'd best go buy a ring, then.'

'Yeah, alright,' I laugh. 'Here, have you heard the news? Something about a riot and someone biting...'

'Caught the tail end of it as I was leaving home. Er, somewhere in Europe, I think...'

'Oh, not here, then?'

'God, no,' he shakes his head, 'storm in a teacup somewhere.'

'Oh.' Losing interest, I put my radio down and start getting ready to go while listening to the night staff gradually filing in, and I smile at the difference in them now.

Three months ago, they were sullen, withdrawn, and stayed in horrible, little cliques. Now I can hear them laughing and sharing jokes while avoiding mentioning the poker game for fear of the late shift staff hearing them.

That's all it is really. We have something the others don't. A secret thing that we can all enjoy with a sense of doing it together. The poker games are only ever for a couple of quid, and the biggest pot ever won was only a fiver.

'Evening!' stepping out the office, I call down to the men and women gathered by the lockers, getting a chorus of replies in return. Happy people smiling and joking, and it almost makes me want to stay at work. Almost.

'Mr Howie.' Turning around to see Dave, one of the night shelf stackers standing there.

'Dave, how are you?' I don't bother trying to correct him calling me Mr Howie. I've said it to him loads of times, but he still does it.

'Fine, thank you, Mr Howie,' he nods briefly, then walks past towards his locker.

'Dave, we had a meeting today. Performance is up, wastage and everything bad is down, so er...' He stares at me with a completely blank face. 'Well, the offer is still there if you want to move onto working days.'

'No, thank you, Mr Howie,' he replies dully. A hard-working man, exceptionally quiet, and he never joins in with the banter or jokes. His breaks are kept to a minimum, and even during his hour-long meal break, he takes enough time to eat, and then goes back to work. Mind you, no one ever takes the piss out of him either. He might be small, but something about him discourages stupid comments.

'Okay, well, let me know if you change your mind.'

'Okay, Mr Howie.'

'I'm off tonight.' He stares at me without expression. 'So, er...have a good night.' I smile. He walks off.

Wishing them a pleasant evening and getting some mild, well-meaning abuse for having a night off, I make my way out and start the walk home.

It's a beautiful, warm night, sultry even, and it feels more like somewhere in Spain than the south of England.

Boroughfare is a nice enough town, close to the sea but inland enough to avoid being classed as a resort town. Midsize, and it's the same as anywhere else, with lots of houses surrounding a town centre.

My place is just off the centre. Noisy, but cheap. I have the top half of a house, with a young couple living underneath me. A residential side street with brick built houses and slate roofs. Average as average can be.

The quickest route is through the side streets, but it only shaves a minute off the journey, and the night is lovely, so I walk back through the High Street, watching the crowds of people moving from pub to pub.

It's packed, really busy. I guess the hot weather is drawing everyone into the centre. People laughing and singing noisily makes me think of my sister living in London. Sarah is a PA for one of the big investment banks. She moved there a few years ago. I know she loves the weekend "networking parties" as she calls them.

I kind of feel like I want to join in and be out with the crowds, drinking, having fun. It's not really my scene, though. I'm not fashion-conscious or stylish, and I don't go for whatever the latest trends are.

Twenty-seven and still shy as hell round pretty girls, and it's only been the last few years that my hair has started looking even remotely decent. Dark, curly, too long, and permanently messy. I don't work out or do anything other than work and piss about at home.

Pausing at the door of the pizza place, I spot a fat bloke inside. I've never learnt what his name is, but I know he likes drinking. He comes into the supermarket most weekends, tanked up and swaying while he buys loads of junk food, crisps, chocolate, pies, and frozen chips.

I feel bad calling him the fat bloke as he's a nice man, always polite and jovial, willing to share a joke, and he's never aggressive like some of the drunks are. Looks professional too from the nice suit he's always got on.

It's just one of those things. Time rolls on, and you end

up meeting people time and again until suddenly it's too late to be asking their name.

'Hello, mate,' I say with a grin, joining him at the counter.

'Hi,' he grins and even holds a hand out, 'supermarket man, yeah, hi! How are you?' He's sober but still really friendly, and this early in the evening, I can see his tie is done up properly, and he looks sharp and switched on.

'Fine,' I nod back amiably, 'night off.'

'Good for you, having a pizza, eh? Don't blame you. They're nice here. Have you tried the meat feast?'

'Oh yes,' I give him a knowing grin.

'You enjoy it, then? Working at Tesco, I mean. I heard they look after their managers quite well.'

'Yeah, it's not bad,' I shrug. 'Lucky to have a job these days.'

'True,' he sighs. 'So you out then or off home?'

'Pizza and home for me.'

'Really? Young bloke like you on a Friday night? Come and have a beer with me if you like.' He means it too. Not a fake, polite offer, but a genuine one.

'Nah, thanks anyway.' As much as I'm sure it would be nice, the town centre at weekends really isn't my scene. Too many pumped up lads wearing t-shirts two sizes too small for them, and women screaming into mobiles phones.

We make small talk until the pizzas are handed over in their lovely, warm cardboard boxes, and after exchanging polite farewells, I make my way through the town to the side street and down to my building, and up to my first-floor flat.

Television on, quick change of clothes, couple of cold ones from the fridge, and within minutes of walking in, I'm sat on the sofa, eating the first slice of thick-crust meat feast while flicking through the channels.

I check the movies out first, but they're all old ones I've seen many times. Next, I check for something funny, but again, it's all repeats, dramas, repeats, documentaries, repeats.

Out of sheer desperation, I flick higher through the numbers until I start hitting the news channels and see footage of the riots they mentioned earlier on the radio.

Some of the footage is awful, and I mean awful. Poor quality, grainy, and obviously snatched by low-resolution cameras in poor light.

Some of it, however, isn't awful. Some is high definition and taken by someone using a modern phone, who at least knows how to hold their hand still. Full colour, full audio, and utterly shocking, filming people with awful injuries, wounds to their faces and necks, bleeding, with noses or ears ripped away. The most shocking thing is seeing police officers and people in uniforms fire handguns into crowds of bystanders; then more police officers using shotguns and assault rifles.

Then more footage is showing SWAT teams and riot police deployed onto streets. Shooting and using huge sticks to batter people writhing on the ground. Gunshots and screams in nearly every segment shown. Injuries too, and so much blood. Blue, flashing lights on cars. Sirens warbling, and people running, and as it goes on, so I start to recognise some of the places they are talking about.

Riga in Latvia. Cities in Lithuania and Estonia. Then Poland and the German border towns. Footage from Moscow in Russia. Budapest. Rome. Zurich. Famous land-marks glimpsed in the backdrop. I've never seen anyone being killed before, but right now, it's been shown without censorship, making me flinch and screw my eyes closed. An Italian cop firing a handgun into a group of people running after him. Except they look weird, like stiff-legged and jerky. He still shoots them, and they still keep running.

The other thing I see are people biting each other. Savagely too. Like they're high on some kind of drug and just going nuts, biting into necks and arms, into anything they can reach. It's bloody gross, and just the thought of being bitten by a drug addict repulses me.

What sickens me even more, however, is the sight of the news anchors in obvious glee at having something so meaty and awful to report on. You can see it in their faces, and I bet the notes they are making on the bits of paper in front of them are in preparation for whatever awards news agencies give each other while pausing dramatically, with fingers pushed into ears as they take fresh information in.

When the main news channels show disasters, they seize on one or two bits of footage and loop it over and over while going through their lists of experts to either phone up or get them into the studio.

This is different because I don't see the same bit of footage twice.

The funny thing is that I was quite calm at first, thinking all these places were a billion light years away and just weird, crazy European cultures having a squabble that would never, could never affect this country.

England, however, has a long history with rioters, and it isn't long before I'm starting to think maybe all those council estate kids in London might flare up again and starting looting JD Sports and Argos.

Then the footage starts showing the same things happening in Luxembourg, Belgium, and France.

France? Bloody hell. That's only a few hours away from where I live. Yeah, fair enough, you've got to get a ferry or a train under the channel...the Channel Tunnel. The tunnel that connects France to England.

Shit. The realisation seems to hit across the board, and I watch the news anchors loosen ties and unbutton the top buttons of shirts, or roll their sleeves up.

There's no mistaking the next bit of footage. The bloody Eiffel Tower is in the background, with masses of people running and screaming. More gunshots – pistols first, then the sustained firing of automatic weapons.

Suddenly, the reasons given for it change.

The anchors start talking about pandemics, contagions, and a fast-acting virus spread by airborne particles or transferred by bodily fluids. Time and again, witness reports state people were being bitten to death. Only they didn't stay dead; they got back up and started biting other people.

This isn't the Friday night I expected to be having, slouched back, with my feet on the coffee table.

Instead, I'm on the very edge of my sofa, flicking up and down the channels, trying to see the difference between the news reports, but it's all the same, and when the first channel starts to transmit the technical error message, I don't really pay too much attention but flick past it in a hurry to see the developments.

Then Euronews goes down, and Sky News reports, they are losing contact with outside agencies. BBC News loses satellite connections.

Things start breaking, phone calls drop out, and for the first time in what is probably television history, the news anchors start to panic.

With a shock, I realise it's gone one o'clock in the morning. I've been glued to the television for hours; then it dawns on me just how fast this thing is spreading.

'...still we have received no government updates. This is a

live request for any government official with knowledge or advice to be given to the people of the United Kingdom to make contact with either our news department or any of the main broadcast news agencies.'

Fuck me. They're asking for the government to get in touch, literally asking if anybody is watching to phone them.

Flicking through the channels, the same request is being made live by multiple news anchors as they beg for someone to tell them what to do.

My stomach starts churning, and I feel sick with worry. Sarah, my sister, will be out in some swanky central London wine bar. Paris is only about an hour train ride from London.

I've got to call her and tell her to get home and lock the doors. I grab my phone, but there's no signal. I live right by the town; the coverage here is excellent. I turn it off and back on, hoping it's my phone playing up.

It isn't. Still no signal. Landline, then. I dust the thing off and use my mobile to find Sarah's number, and I'm halfway through before I realise there is no dial tone on the landline. Nothing, just an empty, faint hiss.

I press the clicker down several times, but that makes no difference, and I glance back at the television, with my stomach dropping again at the sight of the blank screen.

Sky News, BBC News, ITV News, all of them gone. Just blank screens from one channel to the next. Even the technical error messages are gone.

What do I do? No mobile, no landline. No contact with anyone. My parents live in the next town along, just a few miles away, but at this time of night, they'll be tucked up in bed. Maybe I should get to them. I bite my bottom lip, trying to think what to do when I hear noise coming from outside. Footsteps. Someone running.

I get to my lounge window and look out to see a guy running from the direction of the town. A big man too by the looks of it, but he's still shifting quickly despite his size. I spot him giving fast, furtive glances behind him like someone is chasing him.

The fat bloke. Definitely him. Running down my street in his smart suit.

Leaning out, I can see several more people running in the same direction; only they are going much faster than he is and gaining quickly, which, in turn, seems to be making him panic more, and even in the streetlights, I can see his face is flushed bright red as he gasps for air. Poor bastard will have a heart attack if he doesn't slow down.

The group's dynamics start screaming out in my head. The way they people chasing him are running stiff-legged and weird, with no clear cohesion to their movements. Just like on the footage, but this is Boroughfare, a small market town in the middle of bloody nowhere. Then I hear the fat bloke whimpering in panic as he snatches a glance behind him.

'HERE,' I yell out, reacting from instinct and start waving my arms to draw his attention as he looks up with an expression of utter terror.

My front door is locked. He won't be able to get through. A couple of quick steps, and I'm out my lounge and into my tiny hallway, opening my flat door. Down the stairs, past the door to the downstairs flat, and I get to the main front door and go out into the street.

I run down the garden path and into the street, waving my arms for him and shouting for him to keep going. They're bloody close to him now. Maybe five or six of them, men and women, and all of them dressed like they've just come from the town.

The next few seconds are a blur as the fat bloke seems to realise he's done for and comes to a sudden stop. A second of nothingness, of near silence, and he turns to see them coming in hard and lashes out with a weak punch, but they dive in as one, ripping him from his feet in the blink of an eye.

The fat bloke screams with a high-pitched wail full of pain that freezes the blood in my veins. I start moving towards him, but even from this distance, I can see the people are tearing at his flesh with their teeth, ripping him apart with their mouths, tearing into his face, neck, and arms. Blood spraying everywhere, soaking their faces.

'WHAT THE HELL IS GOING ON?' an old man in his pyjamas shouts, striding out of his front door. 'I'M BLOODY SICK OF YOU PISSHEADS FIGHTING EVERY NIGHT.'

The speed they move with from the fat bloke to the old man is frightening, like a pack of animals that want the fresh meat instead of the carcass on the ground, and they burst up and into him with the same frenzied manner.

I've got to do something. I feel compelled to help, but there's nothing I can do. I start creeping backwards towards my front door, with the overwhelming instinct to go slowly in case they see me.

Lights come on a few doors away from the group, and a thickset man comes flying out the front door in his boxer shorts while brandishing a baseball bat. He doesn't hesitate but goes straight at them, battering them off the old man, with the sickening thuds of wood beating hard into skulls.

He gets some good shots, really good shots. The sort of shots that would see the average person going to hospital with a fractured skull, but they don't flinch, and within seconds, he's off his feet and on the ground too. I didn't see his wife come out, but there she is, phone in hand while she screams at them to leave him alone. She even tries grabbing one of the attackers to pull him away, but he launches up to bite into her face. She holds her ground, and for a second, the pair of them stagger around while thrashing violently until her legs give out, and she drops as more join in, biting at her legs and arms while screams and howls fill the air, and yet more people rush from their homes, with lights coming on all up and down the street.

I stop at my gate, transfixed at the sight, frozen in utter shock of seeing people running out from houses, clutching phones as they scream and shout before being taken down amidst trashing limbs. Confusion everywhere. Instant chaos, and I spot a blood-soaked man stagger up the path of a house and in through the open front door, followed by awful screams a few seconds later.

Movement to my right, and I snap my head over to see the fat bloke going from prone to upright in what must be his first sit-up in fifteen years. He gets slowly and awkwardly to his feet, then staggers about; his legs heavy and awkward. Blood streaming down his face, and as he turns towards me, I get the creeping realisation of how utterly stupid I am.

I just watched hours of footage of people being bitten to death and getting back up, and here I am, gawping like a bloody fool at the fat bloke's head lolling about in a jerky manner and his arms hanging loosely at his side like he's got no control over his fine motor skills. Then he finally turns to face me, and I see the red, bloodshot eyes in the sodium streetlights as his lips pull back to show his teeth.

That does it, and I leg it away, sprinting for my front

door as Simon, my downstairs neighbour, comes out of his flat.

'What's going on?' He looks half asleep, dressed in tracksuit bottoms, with no top on.

'Get back inside,' I whisper urgently.

'What's up with you?' he asks. 'What's going on?'

'Get the door shut and keep your voice down.'

'Don't tell me what to do,' he snaps. I've not had much contact with my neighbours Simon and Laura, but what little I've had has left me thinking the bloke is a bit of a prick.

'Mate, seriously, close the fucking door.' I glance back while Simon keeps a firm grip on the handle of the outer door, refusing to let me shut it.

'Are you drunk?' he asks, scowling at me.

'No! Close the fucking door.'

'Simon, I'm trying to sleep,' Laura appears in the doorway of their flat in her bra and knickers.

'Howie's pissed,' Simon says, as though it explains everything.

'No, I'm bloody not,' I reply, still trying ineffectually to get the door closed. Thing is, being an average English bloke, I don't want to physically push him away, so we end up playing tug of war with the front door.

'Well, I'm telling the landlord tomorrow,' Laura shouts. 'I've had enough of this...'

'Shut up,' I hiss, turning to see the fat bloke staggering through our shared garden gate.

'Don't you fucking tell my bird to shut up.'

'I'm not your bird, Simon!'

'Oh, fuck...please...get this door shut. He's coming...'

'Who?' Simon asks, looking past me to the garden path

while we swing the door closed and open. 'What, him? What's he gonna do? Sit on ya?'

'Who's he on about?' Laura asks, stepping out to join Simon looking down the path. 'He's covered in blood. 'Ere, mate, you alright? Simon, ask him if he's alright.'

'You alright, mate?' Simon calls out. 'You been hurt?'

'Oh, god,' I murmur, backing away from the door.

'Fucking pussy,' Simon says with a tut, giving me a filthy look as he goes out the door to stand on the garden path. 'Christ, mate, what happened? You get beaten up?'

'Did he get beaten up?' Laura asks. 'Simon, ask him if he got beaten up.'

'I just did.'

'I'll call an ambulance,' she says, disappearing inside her flat before coming back, with her mobile held in front as she jabs her thumb at the screen.

'Simon, get back inside,' I plead.

'Oh, man up,' Laura snaps while staring in frustration at the phone. 'Bloody network's down again...'

'SIMON,' I scream in warning, but it's too late as the fat bloke speeds up and charges with incredible speed for the last couple of metres, giving Simon no time to react, slamming in hard, with his teeth biting into Simon's neck as he screams out, taken off his feet from the weight of the impact and hitting the ground with a sickening thud.

No time to think, and I run towards them, grabbing at the fat bloke in an effort to pull him off, but his sheer weight prevents me doing anything. In desperation, I start beating down on the back of his head as he bites deeper into Simon's neck.

'GO BACK,' I shout as Laura comes running out, screaming in panic. She goes straight for the man attacking

Simon, grabbing at his arms in a vain effort to pull him away.

Growling behind me like the sound of a dog, and I turn fast to see more of them charging across the street towards us.

'Laura, now! GO NOW!' I try pulling her arm, but she lashes out, striking me in the face, sending me staggering back a step. I try again and grab her arm, but she pulls it free, screaming at me to get off, screaming at Simon to get up. Noise everywhere. Howls and screeches; people in agony. A car screeching past, smashing into other cars further up the street. The sounds of breaking glass. Chaos and bedlam, and everything happening so quickly, but within that utter mayhem, I notice Simon has gone quiet and still, with his eyes closed as the fat bloke slowly lifts his head to stare at me through those red, bloodshot eyes and blood pouring down his chin. The blink of an eye. The beat of a heart. More of them coming in through the gate, and Laura still pulling at the fat bloke. There's nothing I can do, and feeling like an utter coward, I get inside and slam the front door closed, catching a glimpse of the attackers lunging at Laura as the door shuts.

I get up into my own flat, locking and bolting the door before moving into the lounge to stare down out the window.

The sight is incredible and will stay with me forever.

Laura on her back, wearing just bra and knickers, with a huge group of people pushing their heads into her body, biting down into any part of her flesh they can access: legs, arms, neck, torso. One even bites deep into the top of her breast, tearing a chunk of flesh away. If she screams out, I don't hear it, and in shock, I look up and out to see my street looks like a war zone, like a huge movie set.

Bodies all over the place, and people running about, screaming, and being chased. Several get taken down as more of the attackers start charging into front doors. The screams and wails of women and children mix with the deeper, harsher tones of men.

Then another noise comes to the fore, and I look back down to hear the flesh being ripped and torn from Laura's body. Like dogs eating a bone. Gnashing, growling, wet sucks, and tears.

The first heave comes without warning, and the vomit propels from my mouth onto the ground below, hitting with a wet splat. Half-digested pizza, beer, and bile all mixed in, burning my throat and making my eyes water.

I drop to my knees and heave the rest of my guts onto my lounge carpet. Retching and gasping for air, with tears stinging my eyes.

Minutes go by. Long minutes. My throat burns. My head spins, and then finally, I kneel up and peer down to a sea of red, bloodshot eyes staring up at me.

CHAPTER TWO

'Bollocks,' I mutter at the sight. What do I do? Shit. Shit, shit, shit.

Grabbing a coffee mug from the low table behind me, I go back to the window and pull my arm back, which just splashes the cold coffee in my face and makes me yelp in fright while staggering about for a second before I launch the mug hard at the old man in the pyjamas. It hits him straight in the face, knocking him back onto his arse.

I look for something else to throw. The remote control for the television is the closest object, so that gets launched out too and smacks Laura on the shoulder, but she doesn't flinch. I don't even think of how the hell she's back on her feet after being chomped on by so many people.

Instead, I grab anything within reach. Books, DVD cases, even an empty vase gets launched hard and hits a woman on the head, shattering into fragments. She goes down, and I watch in horror as more of them walk over the broken glass, the shards lacerating their feet, but they don't stop moving.

Missiles get launched one after the other, doing nothing

whatsoever to stop them as the flimsy, cheap outer front door gives way, and they start pushing into the communal hallway.

'Cock it!' I run back to my flat door to make sure it's locked, but it's cheap and flimsy too. This is southern England. Doors don't need to be fortified. Arse. 'Barricade,' I mutter the word as the idea pops into my mind and look about for something to use, but my hallway is small, with no furniture.

Into my bedroom, and I grab my bedside drawers to carry back, putting them behind the front door before standing back to proudly view my barricade. One small chest of drawers.

Maybe I need more. Howls and screeches from the other side. Thumps as they run up the stairs.

I definitely need more.

Into the lounge, and I sweep the flat-screen television off the solid, wooden cabinet and start to drag it towards the door, but the DVD player and satellite box are still in the cabinet, plugged into the wall. The cabinet refuses to budge, the wires taut and holding. I open the glass doors and yank them out, forcing the leads to break while I swear foully under my breath.

The cabinet is stacked behind the door, and I spend the next few seconds trying to position the chest of drawers on top of it before realising that one cabinet and one chest of drawers won't be stopping anyone.

The coffee table is added, and I keep going, dragging or carrying whatever I can find. I even get my heavy double mattress and stuff that into the pile. It's not great, but it will slow them down, and it's about all I can do.

I head back into the lounge and look out with a gasp of frustration at the huge crowd pushing beneath my windows.

All of them pushing forward, trying to get to the front door, groaning, hissing, howling, and screeching.

There must be dozens of them, crowding towards the front of the building, and more coming from across the street.

Nothing else for it, so I go back to missile launching. I look around and see my old DVD player on the floor, pick it up, raise it high, then slam it down into the middle of the crowd as hard as I can. It smashes into the head of one of them. I can't tell if it is a man or a woman, but I see them go down, and the space is quickly filled as they all push forward again.

Then I do the same again with the satellite receiver box, smashing it down into the middle of the crowd.

In the kitchen, I spot the kettle. It is an electric, stainless steel one, nice and heavy. I grab it and start back to the lounge, stopping after a few steps to turn back to the kitchen, where I fill the kettle with water and switch it on, then grab everything I can. Pans, plates, cups, bowls, the sugar and coffee pots, and the bread bin. All of them ferried into the lounge to be dumped by the open window.

Back and forth I go until the kitchen fills with steam, making me realise I'd forgotten to put the lid on when I filled the kettle. Grabbing at it too hard, I splash hot water onto my hands, scalding my skin, which just makes me swear even more.

Back at the window, and I slowly pour the hot water down onto the upturned faces, watching as the water sizzles onto bare skin, sending small clouds of steam up, which has absolutely no effect other than washing some of the blood from them.

In desperation, I raise the kettle above my head and

throw it down as hard as I can. It strikes with a loud whack, and another body drops out of sight.

Yeah, that's better, much better. *Blunt trauma beats hot water.*

I take a heavy ceramic pot from the pile and throw it down hard. It strikes a shoulder, and the impact is enough to make the body stumble and fall from view, trampled underfoot as the space is quickly filled.

A frying pan is next, and I launch it down. It hits one on the head with a metallic dong.

It's like shooting fish in a barrel. I've never been in a fight or caused physical injury to another person before in my life, but I am now. I'm slamming down everything I can find and watch as they impact on the heads beneath me.

Some shots are good. The toaster was great, nice and heavy, and straight onto the bald head of a man – he goes straight down, but again, the space is quickly filled.

I keep going, fury and anger driving me to scream abuse at the ragged faces, but within minutes, my pile is diminished, and the front garden is littered with household objects while still more of them stagger in.

I run back to my hallway and stare at the door, listening to the loud bangs and noises coming from the other side. The door rattling in the frame, and the first sounds of wood starting to break are soon heard. They'll be through in minutes, and even my super awesome barricade won't stop them. I have to get out.

My bedroom and lounge both look out over the front. I could probably get down, but there's too many of them outside. I'll be dead within seconds. Maybe the back, then? I run into my kitchen, then the bathroom, shouting in anger at seeing the windows are too small to climb through.

I search for anything left to throw, and my gaze falls

onto the gas hobs as I think about the hot water. Then I remember reading books about medieval times when they poured hot oil from castles onto the invaders.

Finding a bottle of vegetable oil in the cupboard gives me a small sense of victory before I realise all my saucepans are now in the front garden. I have nothing left to use to heat the oil. My microwave is still there, but I have no pots or bowls.

I could lob the microwave at them. It's nice and heavy and might drop one, but what good would that do against so many?

A sense of doom comes over me as I head back into the lounge and over to the window. My lighter is still in the corner of the sill, taunting me. I gave up smoking a few weeks ago as I was getting hard looks from the senior managers every time I popped out for a smoke. Jesus, I could do with a smoke right now.

I might not have any cigarettes, but I have got alcohol, and maybe that will lessen the horror of what's to come. I head into the kitchen and reach up for the bottle of brandy on top of the fridge, and give thanks that I didn't think to grab it in my hunt for missiles.

I take the bottle back to the lounge window and look out as I lift the bottle to drink it straight. Taking a big glug, then grimacing from the harsh bite hitting my throat. Jesus, it's like paint stripper.

One thought leads to another, and I stare at the bottle with fresh interest. Brandy is flammable.

I could use it like a Molotov cocktail... It might burn the house down, but I'm pretty much dead already – it's only a matter of time before they get in.

I dash into the bedroom and tear some strips from my pillowcase, stuffing them into the brandy bottle to soak the amber liquid up. I've seen this done in movies and feel confident of how to do it – you light the end and throw the bottle. What could be easier?

At the lounge window, I hold the bottle, with the brandy-soaked strips of material dangling limply from its mouth and light the end, grinning evilly as the flames take hold.

'Have some brandy, fuckers ...'

My cool and witty one-liner becomes a yelp as the wick bursts into flames, making me panic and throw the bottle down into the crowd. It hits one on the head and bounces off to roll about unbroken, cushioned by the stupid fat head that it struck on the way down.

That's it. My last good idea cocked up. But within a few seconds, I see smoke coming up from the crowd, then a whooshing noise, with flames licking up between the bodies, and I watch as the flames keep rising up. Not that they pay any attention or even try to move away. Even when a couple of them set on fire, with the flames climbing up over their clothes.

The stench of burning flesh hits my nose, making me gag and move away from the window as thick, black smoke billows up into the lounge, carrying that smell of cooking meat. I cough and retch again, heaving on my knees once more, puking bile.

A faint noise penetrates the sound of my coughing. A car horn and coming closer by the sound of it. Lurching to the window, I try and look out, but the smoke is too much, so I go into the bedroom and pull the curtains down to see an armoured cash-in-transit security van in the middle of the road.

I open the window as the horn sounds out again, loud and clear in the still night air, and the reaction is swift as the

infected people in my garden jerk round and start staggering towards it.

'HERE, OVER HERE,' I lean out the window,
screaming and waving at the van in the road as it rolls
forward a few feet while sounding the horn on and off, with
a line of infected stumbling and jerking after it.

They stream out of my garden, and I hear the thumps as
they go down the stairs, then appear, running up the path
and out into the street, with more of them staggering from
houses and appearing in the night, and within seconds,
there's a massive crowd of them.

The van stops and seems to wait for them to get close;
then the reverse lights come on, and the van goes backwards
at speed, slamming into the dense crowd, causing a backwards ripple effect. Then the van shoots forward again,
sounding the horn, leading them on and away like the Pied
Piper.

Within minutes, the street has cleared.

CHAPTER THREE

I wait at the window, listening to the noise from the van ebbing away. Stunned and silent, the after-effects of the excitement and adrenaline making my hands tremble as I rub my face.

I can't stay here; it isn't safe. They have gone for now, but they could come back.

No phones. No way of calling for help, and this, whatever this is, is happening everywhere. That makes me realise the police won't be rushing to my rescue any time soon.

My parents have a detached house in a nice, quiet area. They always go to bed early, and I know they lock the doors, so maybe they're okay. I don't stand a chance of getting to London, not right now anyway. Fuck it. I hope to hell my sister is okay, but right now, all I can do is get to my parents' house.

I look at my watch. It's almost 4.30 a.m. Being mid-July, the sun will be up in half an hour or so. I need to get moving while I've got a chance. I don't own a car, so unless I can find something to drive, I will have to walk.

In the hallway, I stand, staring at the barricade. I don't know if any of them are left out there, and I'm too scared to remove the barricade and look.

I go into my bedroom and pull a couple of sheets from the airing cupboard, then tie them together with a duvet cover. I go to the window and look outside to make sure it's still clear, then tie one end onto the leg of my double bed, and drop the sheets down. They reach to a couple of feet above the ground.

Weapon. I need a weapon if I'm going out there. I root through the kitchen drawers to find my biggest carving knife with a nice, sharp, pointed blade.

I put the knife into my belt, with the blade resting against my leg. Then an image of me lying on my back, with the knife sticking in my leg fills my mind. I need a sheath, but kitchen knives don't have sheaths.

I find the small rucksack that I use for work and put the knife into the main compartment, leaving the top open, and I try to wedge the knife into the top zip so that the handle is left out, with the blade in the bag.

I put the bag on my back, but it hangs down too low – I can't reach the handle. I tighten the straps and raise the bag further up my back so I can reach back with my hand and grasp the handle.

An old claw hammer is added to my pathetic arsenal, but at least I have something that I can use. I think back to the man in boxer shorts hitting them with a baseball bat. He hit them hard, and they got knocked away, but they came back. So I know that hitting them won't kill them, but maybe it will buy me a few seconds to run.

I go back to the bedroom window and start to climb over the sill, grasping the bed sheets with both hands. I wait, sitting astride the window ledge, listening, and looking up and down. No noise and no movement. The night's veil is just starting to lift. Only a few minutes until sun is up. I don't know if that is a good thing or not.

I need to go, but I'm bloody terrified, and the final act of leaving the safety of my home is almost too much for me to contemplate.

Staying here isn't an option. They could come back, and my front door won't take another battering, and so, while shaking with fear, I clamber over the ledge and start lowering myself with my hands.

I feel extremely vulnerable, with my legs dangling beneath me, and I keep looking around, imagining that one of them will come out of the door, so I run into the road, with the hammer out of my waistband and in my hand.

The sight is worse at ground level. The micro-detail so very much worse as I get a close-up of the frenzied attack. Blood stains are everywhere, and a white car parked just a few feet away has bloody handprints smeared across the bonnet and a corpse trapped under one of the front wheels.

A crash behind me, and I see one of the things stagger out from my front door. That's enough for me. I'm off, giving it billy big legs, sprinting until I feel my lungs will burst, and my legs are hurting. I slow down and look back, but he is gone from sight.

I keep walking fast, sticking to the middle of the road, looking left and right; my ears straining for any noise. The quickest route is straight through town and down the High Street, then onto the dual carriageway.

A few minutes later, I reach a side street that feeds into the town centre and edge forward slowly until I reach the building line. I pause, listening intently and trying to summon the nerve to keep going. I've never been so terri-fied. Why is it so silent? Is that good? My mind starts imagining the infected things are all waiting somewhere, ready to jump out and eat me.

At least the sun is almost up now as the night sky gradually ebbs away. Even the birds are singing, and I spot seagulls flying overhead, calling out in the early dawn.

Come on, Howie. I force courage where there is none and move towards the junction of the High Street, cautious and slow. I step out and see the right is clear, and almost breathe a big sigh of relief until I look left and see an enormous crowd of them gathered around the armoured security van that led them away from my house, now stopped in the middle of the road.

Why did it stop? It hasn't crashed from what I can see. Maybe there were just too many bodies to drive through? I think to run back and start easing away when the hatch on the roof of the van opens, and a man climbs out to stand, looking down at the crowd as they swarm around him like fans at a rock concert.

Then the man looks up and spots me staring over while I stand still, unsure of what to do. 'RUN,' he shouts at me.

I take a step forward, and he shakes his head. 'NO, RUN. RUN NOW.'

I don't know what to do. He saved my life, and I can't just leave him to his death. Maybe I could get a vehicle and do the same as he did – lure them away with the sound of a horn.

I look back at the van and can see that there are hundreds of the things surrounding him, spread out in a wide circle, all pushing forward. The man looks safe enough now, but it won't take long for them to either climb up or use each other to trample on and gain height.

I run down the road to the closest car, but it's locked and secure. This is the town centre, and no one in their right mind would leave a car unlocked here. With a jolt, I see the pizza restaurant further up the road and remember the conversation I had with the fat bloke just a few hours ago.

He was right there, chatting like normal as we ordered food. Dressed in his smart suit and getting ready for a few drinks. The images of his torn flesh flood through my mind, of the blood loss, the arteries opened up, of the horrific noises he made. Pain inside. Other feelings too. Too many of them. Confusion. Denial, even. This can't be happening. It *can't* be real. This stuff happens in movies. Not in real life. Yet here I am, as real as anything. I even blink and look back up the road to see the horde of infected things, and the guy still on the van roof, waving at me to keep going. A surreal moment that makes me pause and hold still as my frazzled brain struggles to process it all.

Then in the middle of that slack-jawed, confused moment, I spot the pizza delivery moped lying on its side outside the restaurant. The distinctive white box on the back, and before I know what I'm doing, I'm running over and wrenching the thing upright, wincing at the sticky blood on the handles.

An old thing with a twist and go grip to keep it simple for the students and teenagers who use it to earn a few extra quid. Thank fuck the key is still in the ignition.

I wheel the moped out into the road and wave up to the guy on the roof of the van a few hundred metres away. I point at the moped and gesture that I'll drive away and try to get them to follow me. He shouts back and waves, maybe trying to tell me something, but the distance is too great to hear the words.

I get on the moped and turn the keys to the off position and then back on before pressing the start button as the moped splutters noisily to life. The loud noise so familiar to me from all of the times I have had takeaway delivered and heard the moped coming up the street.

As the sun rises, and daylight fills the street, I look back to the van, expecting the infected people to be already coming for me as my hand readies to twist and go, and lead them away, but something is different.

The outer ring of the crowd has turned and started towards me, but they are moving slower, much slower. Shuffling and dragging their feet. They were fast and wild just a few minutes ago, like predators after prey, relentless and sustained. Now they are stumbling as if they are walking through deep water; each step a struggle.

I look all about, fearing some kind of trap, but they are all the same. Some are turning and heading my way; others remain standing around the van, and whereas before they had a menacing aura, now they are a stumbling mess. The steps they take are thudding, with straight legs and arms hanging limp, and heads lolling about. They keep knocking into each other too, bumping away and going off course, seemingly unable to follow a straight path.

I look to the guy on the van and raise my arms, with the international signal for *what the fuck?*

He raises two arms, palms up, the international signal for *fuck knows*. Then he starts doing something else, waving and gesturing, but I can't get what he means.

I step off the moped and push the stand down with my foot, leaning the bike over to rest in situ, with the engine still running and ready to go.

Taking a couple of tentative steps towards the mass crowd, I watch them move and shuffle. What's happened? Why have they changed?

The crowd is still too thick to attempt a rescue. There are hundreds of them, and only about half are turned in my direction; the rest are still surrounding the van. I need to get them away too.

I go back to the moped and press the horn. A feeble warble sounds out, but I keep my finger pressed down on the button. This appears to focus the direction of their stumbling, and I notice more of the crowd turn away from the van towards my direction.

I keep pressing the horn and twist the accelerator grip, thinking that I will rev the engine, forgetting the bloody thing is twist and go, and the moped shoots forward, pulling me along. In my panic, I twist the grip more, and the moped pulls away faster, with me still hanging on.

The kickstand bangs into the road surface, propelling the moped off to the right. I slip and fall over as the moped veers off and crashes into a parked car with a loud bang before clunking over to the ground; the engine spluttering for a few seconds before it dies out. I scrabble up and twist around to see the horde is still shuffling slowly, and the guy on the van is covering his face with one hand, and even from this distance, I can see him shaking his head.

'I'm okay,' I call out while grinning like a bloody fool, bounding up to my feet as though nothing happened. I run over to the moped and lift it up again. It starts first time, and I wheel it back into the road, pressing the horn and waiting until they get closer. Staring at them and taking in the awful details of the injuries and the blood. At how they are people, but not people.

The closest one is maybe twenty years old and dressed in his designer jeans, with his muscles bulging from his tight top, and his hair all gelled up in the middle in that messy-on-purpose style that I hate. A torn, ragged wound in his cheek flaps open to show rows of teeth, and there is dark red blood all over the front of his once white t-shirt and down his arms. There is also a dark stain across the crotch of his blue jeans, but it doesn't look like blood. He must have pissed himself when they got him, which makes me feel better. I was terrified, but at least I didn't wet myself.

I'm not much older than him, but I've always hated the weekend town centre crowds. Preening, strutting fuckwits. My hair is curly and always messy without the need for gels and sprays.

I think back to the times when I had been out in the town at weekends, getting barged into by idiots like this, who flared up, with their arms puffed out.

I've always worked. Maybe it isn't the best job, but I've held it down and made duty manager, and I know that if I do the hated night shifts, there will be a chance for promotion.

No, there *was* a chance for promotion, but that's gone now. It's all gone ... Everything has gone. Jesus. This is it. I saw it happen on the news. Every country. Everywhere. I saw it happen in my own street, and how fast it can spread. The end of the world. There's no going back from something like this. Not now.

A deep sense of sadness fills me, and I start breathing hard as I think of my workmates being savaged by monstrous, preening pretty boys like this. They were always coming into the supermarket at night, especially after the clubs had kicked them out, throwing stuff about and taking the piss out of the staff.

I think about the fat bloke and the life he must have led. Maybe he was deeply sad at his obesity. A reject from society like the rest of us, but he was polite and friendly, and always willing to stop and exchange a few pleasantries, and he never looked down his nose at us either.

I look up and watch the pretty boy, with a weird anger

rising up inside. Anger like I have never known before. I can feel my breathing becoming deeper and harder, my heart hammering in my chest. A feeling I have never had before. Consuming my mind. Something in me snaps, with a feeling of such ferocity it drives my actions without conscious thought, and before I know it, I've drawn the hammer from my waistband, stepped forward, and smashed the hard metal end into the side of his head. He drops instantly, and I go down too, pounding the hammer into his head, shattering his face, and crushing his skull, driving the blunt-ended weapon into his head. Blood and brain matter spray up and coat my arms. My hands become slick and glistening; terror and rage mixing into a deadly cocktail. All reason is gone.

I stop suddenly, becoming alert to my actions. What is left at my feet is not recognisable. The head is pulped, gone, destroyed. I destroyed it. I killed it. I killed one of them, and my chest heaves as I struggle for air and stagger backwards.

A sudden movement to my right; another one lunging at me, and in reflex, I lash the hammer out in a backswing as it leans in with teeth bared. The force drives the thing off to the side, spinning into a woman wearing a nice, blue dress. Full-figured, with a heaving cleavage, and long, brown hair, but her face is slack, and her eyes are filled with blood.

She staggers toward me, leaning forward from the waist. Lips now pulled back and ready for the bite. I feel repulsed and step backwards while thinking it's wholly wrong to hit a woman. That's how I was raised from a child. You never hit a woman.

I blink and move away a step as I look at the woman. She appears uninjured, without a bite mark or blood on her until I look down and see a chunk of muscle in her right thigh has been bitten away.

A groan from my left, and a young man with tribal tattoos all over his arms and neck shuffles in, then lunges as though surging to bite. I lash out and slam the hammer into the side of his face. He goes down hard but keeps moving, and rolls onto his back before sitting up. I strike him again harder, and I see his head snap to one side as he's flung over and feel, and hear the crunch of bone in his cheek breaking. Yet, within seconds, he's back to sitting up.

I spin the hammer round so that the claw end is now the weapon and drive it down into the top of his skull, cleaving through the bone. The force I use pushes the claw into his skull too hard, and it sticks. I try pulling it out, but all I do is pull him towards me.

I put my foot onto his chest and pull harder, and the strength of my pull forces his body into my foot. I stagger backwards and fall down; the hammer left sticking out the top of his head, at which point I become aware of just how close they all are now and still shuffling in. Every one of them staring directly at me, and hundreds of pairs of red, bloodshot eyes watching my every move. Groans sounding out. Feet shuffling. Bodies moving.

Then the sight of the fat bloke snatches my breath away. He's right there, waddling along, with the rest of them as he staggers towards me. Pretty boy is on the ground right in front of him, yet the fat bloke goes straight over him, trudging his big feet over the corpse. Fast, conflicting emotions course through me. Just seconds ago, I felt an over-whelming sense of shame and guilt at the anger, which drove me to kill that thing.

My fingers scrabble for the zip to the bag's main compartment. I get my hand in and feel the plastic handle, and pull the long kitchen knife out.

Still moving backwards, I look at the shiny blade, then at the mass of infected people, then back to the blade.

'Fuck this,' I mutter.

I'm off, running away as I throw the knife off to one side, then regret the action immediately. I go back, grab the knife, and start running again.

Towards the end of the street, I slow down and look back to see the top of the armoured van is empty.

I scan about for a few seconds, but I can't see him. There is just a mass of infected people on a slow march like a zombie protest through the town.

I keep moving, and after a few minutes, I see a mountain bike with no lock propped up against a wall. I grab the bike and start pedalling like crazy down the High Street and onto the main road, leaving the crowd far behind.

CHAPTER FOUR

I know it's still very early in the morning, but there would normally be delivery trucks, milkmen, commuters, all slowly emerging as the day wakes up.

Now there is nothing. It's so quiet. One of the pedals starts to squeak with each rotation of the cog, and it's that single noise that keeps me company on the quiet road.

I haven't cycled in a long time, and it doesn't take long before my thigh muscles are hurting.

My life consisted of working all night, then sleeping in the day, eating crappy food, and drinking too many beers in front of the television. I'm paying for it now as I feel exhausted and drained.

My parents' house is a fifteen-minute drive away from mine. How long will it take to cycle to them?

I try to work it out. A car going at about thirty miles per hour would take fifteen minutes, so if I cycle at fifteen miles per hour, it will take me half an hour.

I have no idea what speed I am doing, but it must be at least fifteen miles per hour; then I try to remember what speed normal walking pace is. I'm sure it was on TV once …

I think it was four or five miles per hour, and I reckon I am going much faster than walking pace.

My arse hurts, and my legs are on fire, feeling weird and pumped up. I think ahead, trying to choose the route I should take. One takes me through the side streets, residential roads with houses, and the other would take me on the motorway. Cycles are not allowed on motorways, so I would be breaking the law, whereas the alternative would take me via the houses and all the things lurking about.

I think I'll risk being arrested. In fact, being arrested would be the best thing in the world right now. A nice, safe cell in a locked police station.

The squeaking pedal and I cycle down the junction and onto the motorway.

It's still early but hot as hell, and the sweat is pouring from my face. I hold the bike steady with one hand while I pull the bottom of my t-shirt up and start wiping the stinging sweat from my eyes and face.

A noise from behind – a car engine, loud and fast. I drop my hand to look back over my shoulder and see a red car coming up behind me; the engine screaming out into the quiet air. I immediately put my hand up and start waving.

I'm in the outside lane, closer to the middle section, which is the same as the car, and it's coming bloody quickly, so I start to move over towards the middle. The car does the same, so I start swerving back to the outside lane, but again, it changes course. For a second, it feels like the car is aiming for me, but at the last second, it swerves to the side and goes stonking past at such a high speed the slipstream causes me to wobble. I catch a glimpse of a woman driving. Then as it pulls ahead, I see someone in the back seat, but it looks weird, like the passenger is lurching forward to speak to the driver.

Then the car veers off and strikes the safety barrier with a loud crash. The speed so great and the angle of impact so hard, it immediately flips the back end up and out, causing the vehicle to roll over and over in the air. The noise is incredible – a thudding, awful boom, followed by near on silence as the vehicle sails for long seconds before crashing back down to earth. Rolling with terrible, wrenching, metallic screams. Glass imploding, and a whole wheel shorn off to go bouncing down the road. Debris flying far and wide, and the vehicle scoring a long, deep gouge in the tarmac before it comes to rest on its roof.

All is instantly quiet again, apart from the squeaking of my pedal as I cycle faster towards the wreck.

The car is utterly destroyed. The front end is crumpled in, and the remaining front wheel looks buckled. The windows have shattered into thousands of tiny pieces glittering on the road, and I catch scent of burning rubber mixed with chemicals in the air, petrol too.

As I give a final burst of speed, I hear a loud crunch and feel a sudden loss of pressure from the pedals. The chain snaps audibly and twangs off to snarl into the rear wheel, which causes me to lose control. I squeeze the brakes and steer to the right to avoid a collision, but the bike hits some of the liquid, and the back tire loses grip, causing me to fall off and slide along the debris-strewn road.

How is that possible? How is it possible that on an empty motorway, I fall off my bike to smash into the only pissing car here?

Noises coming from the car snap me back to reality, and I'm up, scrambling towards the driver's window as a slender arm drops out, the fingers clenching into a fist.

'Fuck!' The movement makes me jump back, fearing one of those things is about to come flying out at me.

'Help!' a female voice, low and weak, and I go lower onto my stomach, crunching over broken glass to see a woman with blonde hair upside down being held in place by the seatbelt as the deployed airbags sag down at her sides and from the steering wheel.

'Hey! Are you hurt?'

She snaps her head over, staring at me with relief through normal, blue eyes filling with tears.

'I'll get you out, okay? My name's Howie. Can you move?'

I try to remember what should be done now. She could have a neck or spinal injury, so should stay still until the emergency services get here. Only there aren't any emergency services now. No firemen to cut the roof off, and no paramedics to get her onto a spinal board.

Fluids are still leaking from the car; the pungent stench of fuel and chemicals. Can it explode like they do in movies?

'I'm going to pull you out,' I say it as gently as I can, but there really isn't any choice. She has to get out of the vehicle.

'Okay,' she replies quietly, obviously shocked. Grasping her hand, I start applying pressure, but out of fear of hurting her, I don't pull hard enough, then realise the seatbelt is still on.

'The seatbelt, can you undo it?' She looks at me, then slowly turns her head to grope for the clasp. 'Hang on,' I say, fearing she will fall on her head. I lie flat on my back and push my hands up against her shoulders. 'Okay, do it now,' I say and hear the click as she pushes the button down and drops on my head.

'Sorry,' she gasps from somewhere on top of me.

'S'fine,' I say, somewhat muffled as we wriggle and

writhe, with poky bits of broken car digging into our bodies. I slide out of the wreck and twist around to start pulling her out by her arms as she seems to revive a bit, with colour and life coming back into her face.

'Just...a bit...further,' I say as she slowly comes out of the mangled window.

'Okay... Keep going...' she replies, her voice a little stronger now.

'Does your back hurt?'

'No. I think I'm okay.'

'Thank god for that. What about the other person?' I ask tentatively, thinking the person in the back might not have survived.

'Gordon!' she gasps as her upper body is pulled free and stares up at me before letting go with an ear-piercing scream. I drop her in panic as she starts thrashing about violently. 'MY LEG! MY LEG!'

'What the...' I blink and swallow, my heart once more going like the clappers as I drop down and edge in closer, thinking there must be a shard of metal stuck in her leg. 'Let me see. Please just...'

'MY LEG! MY FUCKING LEG!'

Wiggling closer, I try and get a view of the inside, then spot the back of a man's head moving in the gap between the seats.

'I think he's alive,' I shout, my words trailing off with sick realisation at the same time as he lifts his head up to show his mouth dripping with blood from the hole he has bitten into the back of her calf muscle. He growls once like a dog, then sinks back down to bite again, causing a fresh burst of agonising screams.

'Fuck!' Pushing myself out of the vehicle, I get free and grab her wrists. 'Hold on,' I say through gritted teeth. She screams in complete agony but slides free from the car. With her leg shifted, the man immediately starts writhing towards the gap left by her exit.

A quick glimpse shows me that one of his arms has been removed at the shoulder joint, shorn clean off, with thick blood pumping out. Even in the midst of such carnage, I can't help but notice the blood flow is nowhere near what I would expect. It falls out in thick globules rather than pulsing out in a stream.

'My leg...fuck! It hurts... Oh...fuck...it hurts...' she screams in agony.

I look down at her leg and the blood pouring out from the wound. The bite must be down to the bone. I need to stop the bleeding, but I don't have any bandages. I take the belt off of my jeans and start to wrap it around her thigh.

'We've got to stop the bleeding,' I say.

'Okay,' she gasps. Glancing up, I figure that the man inside the car is moving slowly enough to give us time.

Wrapping the belt around her thigh, I thread it back through the loop and start cinching it tight as she stares down at the wound. 'I'm bleeding out,' she gasps. 'Pull it.'

I wrench back on the belt, trying to form a tourniquet, but the muscles in her thighs are too hard. She still screams out from the pain and starts clutching her belly too, writhing in agony.

'Shit, I'm so sorry!' Dropping down again, I loosen the belt and push it further up her thigh, feeling very awkward at seeing her smooth expanse of skin and her knickers. 'God, I'm so sorry, so sorry.'

'It's okay...' she says, her voice ragged and harsh. 'Do it, just fucking do it.'

Wrapping the belt round again, I pull on the free end

and gradually apply more pressure. I stare down at the pulsing wound, but there is no change.

'Fucking pull it, then,' she growls. I heave with all my strength as she screams out. Her hands reaching up to grab at my arms. I pull the belt harder and harder, and I even get my foot onto her thigh for leverage as I cinch it tighter into her flesh.

'Almost,' I pant and keep going, determined to get enough pressure so the blood stops coming out. If I can stop the blood flow, I can dress the wound and try releasing the tourniquet a bit; maybe it will clot on its own. Fuck it, I should have signed up for the advanced first aid course.

She falls silent as I slowly ease my grip, and the belt holds in place. The bleeding now much less than it was.

'I've done it,' I say hoarsely.

No response. I twist round to see she has gone quiet, like she's asleep. Her hands out to the sides.

'Hey! Hey! Wake up,' I gently move her head but get no response. Tapping the side of her face, I try and wake her. Still no response. I lower my head so that my ear is next to her mouth, and I can feel very soft breath on my cheek.

A groan sounds behind me from the infected man trying to crawl out of the car, stretching his remaining arm out towards us. I rush in and drive my right foot down onto his head, sending a jolt up through my leg, but I keep going, stamping over and over as he gargles and snaps his mouth. I aim for the neck and finally feel a crack under my foot.

Hobbling back to the woman, I drop down to rest my ear against her mouth. There's no breath this time. 'Wake up. Come on. Please wake up,' I plead, feeling for a pulse in her neck, but there is nothing. I try her wrist. No sign of life. I lift her eyelids. I don't know what I am looking for, but they always do this in the movies. It must be the pupils; to see if they dilate. There is no movement, just blank eyes looking a bit bloodshot.

In desperation, I lower the side of my head to her chest, trying to hear a heartbeat. I stay for a few seconds, attempting to calm my breathing so that I can listen properly. Nothing. Just silence. She's dead. I sigh deeply, swallowing and thinking to rise when I hear a single thud, and hold still. Another. Then another. A heartbeat for sure. She's alive.

An explosion of motion, and her arms grab hard, pulling my head into her chest as her heartrate goes nuts, and my world fills with soft breasts squishing into the side of my face, which at any other time would be quite nice.

Not now though, and I try to pull away, but her grip is too strong, and her fingers dig into my scalp, clawing at me. I can't get leverage to move, so I try and prise her fingers from the back of my head, but they are so strong I can't move them.

I can hardly breathe from her boobs going in my mouth and covering my nose, and I start panicking at hearing the growls coming from her throat. God knows how, but I get a hand up into her hair, fix a grip, and yank hard enough to snap her head back, and manage to slip out from under her vice-like grip.

I fall back, rolling away and catching sight of her eyes now horrifically red and bloodshot. Her lips pulled back, showing me her perfect, white teeth, with drool spilling out, and no sign whatsoever of the person I just tried to save. Nothing. No recognition. Just an animalistic beast snapping its mouth open and shut.

'Fucking bitch! You fucking bitch!'

I get to my feet and kick her in the face, then do it again, pulling back like a footballer, ramming my foot into her nose. I feel the bone crunch, and her head snaps back. Terror grips me. I'm in shock from seeing her die and come back, but what came back wasn't the same as the woman that died. My foot slams into her face again and again, and she takes a remarkable amount of blows before she finally lays still.

I stagger away, with my hands to my head, deeply in shock. My vision blurring, and hot tears stinging my eyes. The shorn-off wheel on the ground, the buckled vehicle upside down amongst the glittering shards of glass, and the pooling liquids mixing with the blood from the two dead bodies. The two bodies I killed.

That woman was alive in my arms, pleading for me to save her life. She spoke to me, and we shared something. Maybe only a few seconds in time, but we shared a connection. Two living people. She was alive and spoke to me, and I failed. I failed to save her.

If I hadn't fallen off that bike, if I had got up quicker and moved faster, and if I had pulled hard enough the first time, I might have saved her, but I didn't do those things, and she died.

It's my fault. She looked at me, spoke to me; we made eye contact, and I told her that I would help her.

The sickening action of kicking her replays in my mind – the image of my foot connecting with her face. This is awful; the most awful thing I have ever done, and nothing will ever be the same again.

I tried to save her, and I failed.

But then she came back and was attacking me. The strength in her hands and arms was incredible. She turned and became infected or whatever those things are, and I had to stop her, didn't I?

My mind whirls as I try to make sense of what's

happening, justifying the actions to myself, reasoning, and rationalising. If I didn't kill her, she could have got me or someone else. But we're in the middle of a motorway, with no one else nearby. Who could she have hurt? Did I kill her through defence, or was it murder, with an act of vengeance, carried out through fear and rage?

I have to change this thought process. She was not a *she* when I kicked her; she was infected. One of them.

The woman from earlier on was not a young lady out for the evening, getting excited about wearing her new, low-cut, blue dress. She was not a *she*. *It* was infected, and *it* wanted only to make me the same as them.

The quicker I get that into my head, the safer I will be, and the greater chance for survival I will have.

I lower my hands from my head, resolute, changed, and hardened.

I walk away without looking back.

CHAPTER FIVE

Half an hour, and I'm still on the motorway, with fields on both sides. I haven't seen or heard anyone, and with the adrenalin all gone, I feel totally and utterly drained.

I need to find a vehicle. Walking will take too long, but then there isn't exactly a good supply of cars on the motorway. I see houses in the distance over the fields and clamber over the crash barrier and down a ditch to cross the land.

After the smooth surface of the motorway, the field is uneven and hard going. It looks to be pasture (I think that's what they call it), the type of land that animals graze on. I realise that I have no idea what different types of land there are or what different crops look like, or even if they can be eaten or not. I work in a supermarket, selling produce all day. We get training on certain things so that we can sound convincing to the customers and increase sales, but I can't remember anything useful.

The field borders a lane, which I follow into the village. The first few houses are detached and large, but gradually they get closer together until a pavement starts running down both sides.

I reach the junction into the village and realise I've been here a few times before. Normally when the motorway was closed off, or my dad wanted to take the scenic route. I know there's a garage workshop at the end of the main road. Hopefully, they'll have something I can use.

I keep to the middle of the road, passing open front doors, which look creepy in the silence. Blood on the ground too. Huge, wet stains like someone was brought down here and bled out, but there is too much blood to have just been from one person. Then again, the human body has something like eight pints of blood in it. I try to imagine what eight pints poured onto the floor would look like; probably like that woman back on the motorway.

Then I spot a white UPVC door smeared with blood, and the more I look, the more of it I see. On windows. On doorsteps. Splashed up walls and across kerbs. Sinister and terrible. It stinks too, with a metallic tang hanging in the hot air.

This was a mistake. I should have stayed on the motorway.

I reach the small collection of shops on the right, opposite a small village square, where we used to park to visit the cake shop, and as I get closer, I get a feeling of impending doom just before the small square comes into view crammed full of infected people. The same as they were in my town. All of them shuffling and groaning quietly, and all gathered in one place.

I come to a complete stop. There must be thirty or forty of them, dressed in differing styles of nightwear: pyjamas, nighties, pants, knickers, and bras. Some are naked. All of them are covered in blood.

I can't understand why they are all here. Maybe they're gathering from some remaining spark of intelligence drawing them to the heart of the village. I slowly back away one step at a time, watching for any sign that they've seen me.

Behind me, I hear glass bottles being knocked over and spin round to see an infected male shuffling out of a doorway, kicking milk bottles with his feet, making them spin off to shatter on the road.

If I move quickly, I can get past him, but another one comes out of the house opposite, staggering into the road, heading my way as the village square infected people all react from the noise and shuffle round to see me.

'Shit, shit,' I murmur quietly and start back, thinking that I can still make it through the middle of the two behind me, but more come lurching from houses further down the road, blocking my escape route. I turn back to the road ahead, but the village square horde are spilling into the road, coming at me.

I start running for it, aiming for the newsagents while praying that it's open. As I run past the cake shop and the butchers, a quick thought enters my mind of the massive knives and cleavers they would have, but the door is locked and too solid to force quickly. I run on, towards the newsagents.

The horde is across the road ahead of me, coming from my left, slow moving, and I pass them by a few metres as I reach the shop and bounce off the door. I slam at it again, glancing back to the encroaching horde getting closer by the second, and start whacking at the door, begging it to open.

'Shit, come on! COME ON!'

Looking down, I see the word PULL marked clearly on the door in big letters and yank it open, stumbling through, and pull it shut behind me. Slamming the lock in place, I look for bolts, but there are none. Instead, there are two metal hooks meant to hold a bar, but I can't see the bar anywhere.

I move away from the door as the infected get to the other side, banging into the door with loud groans. Their twisted, gruesome faces smearing blood and saliva over the glass panes, but at least they're not launching themselves at it like last night in my flat.

I back away, with my eyes fixed on them and stumble into a shelf full of chocolate bars, and the sight of them makes me realise just how hungry and thirsty I am. I grab a bottle of Lucozade from the chiller cabinet and start guzzling the sweet liquid down before finishing off with a loud belch, and feeling the instant rush of energy spiking inside. A Mars bar. A Snickers. Another Lucozade, and my sugar levels go nuts as my body starts thrumming, and I stuff more into my bag.

That done, I widen my eyes and think of what to do while my heart beats faster from the energy coursing through me. That's when I see the cigarette display behind the counter.

All of the supermarkets have been fitted with sliding metal doors now in a vain attempt by the government to hide cigarettes away. I thought smaller shops were covered by the same laws too.

I did give up smoking, but hey, I'm surrounded by zombies, and civilisation has fallen. Fuck it, time for a smoke.

I take some tobacco and rolling papers. Tailor-made cigarettes are too expensive, so I switched to tobacco some time ago. There was nearly always someone selling duty-free tobacco from their holidays. After smoking roll-ups for so long, I couldn't go back to normal smokes – the taste is disgusting.

I open the packet and roll a smoke, with my hands shaking a little, but it's quickly done, and I use a lighter from a display pack on the counter.

I inhale deeply and feel the nicotine receptors joining the party held by the sugar dudes in my brain. All of which combines to make me feel somewhat lightheaded. Swaying a little, I lower down until my forehead is resting on the cool countertop while listening to the infected groan and bump into the door and windows.

The dizzy spell eases, leaving me with a pleasant buzz, and as I open my eyes, I spot a baseball bat wedged under the counter. 'Thanks very much,' I say into the quietness of the shop and pull the bat out. These shops open early and could be easy targets, especially in the dark winter mornings.

The smoke from the cigarette in my mouth curls up into my eyes, stinging them. I clench my eyes shut and wait for a few seconds before opening them gently and blinking the tears away.

As I focus again, I see someone standing at the back, behind a bead curtain that separates the shop from the private area. He's a big man too, with a fat gut straining against the material of his short-sleeved shirt now covered in blood from the ragged bite wound on his neck.

He moves slowly forward through the bead curtain, with bloodied drool hanging from his mouth, and his horrible, red eyes staring at me while his head lolls about.

I look about for an avenue of escape, but the only way out is through him. Unless I use the main door, which right now doesn't seem a viable alternative.

The shopkeeper shuffles on; his bulk filling the aisle as he heads towards the counter. I stand still and spit the cigarette away to the side, not taking my eyes off him.

As he gets closer, I watch his head lolling back and forth, and to the sides, but all the time, the red, bloodshot eyes stay fixed on me. Then his head hangs down, with his chin to his chest, and he looks up at me, menacing and very scary.

He walks straight to the counter, and I grasp the baseball bat at the base with two hands and slowly twist my upper body off to the right, raising the bat behind me, ready to strike.

We stare into each other's eyes, fixed, unmoving; neither of us blinking, and long seconds go by. His lips peel back to show yellow, uneven teeth. He can just feel the bite. He can visualise sinking his dirty, yellow teeth into my flesh.

I think to say something cool, but nothing comes to mind, so I just hit him in the head with the bat instead. It's a good hit too, and he goes flying off to the side, colliding with some shelves and sending chocolate bars and tins of beans over the floor.

I put the bat down on the counter and pick the heavy till up, yanking it hard to pull the cable free before I raise it above my head and slam it down on the squirming man as he wrestles with the shelving on the floor. The till smashes into his head, and I move out from the counter to see he's now dead. Like properly dead. Like not-coming-back-to-life-from-some-weird-infection dead. Not with his brains leaking out like that anyway. I've never seen brains outside the head before in real life. They look weird, like little sausages all stuck together.

Stepping through the curtain with my bat raised, I see a small stock room and a flight of stairs going up. To the back of the stock room is a door – barred and bolted. I move over to the door and peer through a grimy window to a small backyard and a wall a few feet away. All empty and quiet.

I pull the bolts back, tug the door open, and peer out into the yard. It has a high brick wall and a wooden gate. I go over to the gate, raise the latch, and lean out to see a small, clear road.

Going left will take me towards the garage I was originally heading for, but an idea forms in my mind, and I turn back.

I close the gate quietly, head into the stock room, and shut the back door, pushing the bolt into place.

With the bat raised and ready, I climb the stairs to the flat above the shop and check the rooms.

Once I'm sure it's all clear, I go back down into the shop and find the cans of lighter fluid on display and some nice, big boxes of matches.

Back upstairs. The windows are old sash and already open in this sultry summer weather, and I look down to about fifty infected all gathered at the front of the shop. I have flashbacks to last night when I was trapped and my ham-fisted attempt at making a Molotov cocktail resulted in me puking up. I don't intend to stick around and watch this time.

I pull the little plastic spout on the first one, up-end the can, and squeeze a jet of liquid out onto the crowd below. It takes quite a long time to empty each can, leaning out and bending over to prevent any spraying on me or the windowsill.

I open the box of matches and pause for a second, hardly believing what I am about to do. Mass murder at any other time. I strike a match and flick it out, but it expires before it falls a few feet. I try another, and the same thing happens. The third time, I lean out and brace my feet, ready to pull back in. I extend my arms, strike a match, and shove it into the open box, pushing it into the dark heads of the little sticks. The box flares instantly – a bright light and stench of sulphur. I drop the box and pull myself in, ducking down below the window just before the whoosh hits, and the flames sear up, with black smoke already billowing up.

I risk a quick look out and gawp at the flames spreading quickly, leaping from body to body. Time to go before I puke from the stench, and I'm off, running down through the shop and out the back door, and into the alley with my new bat in hand.

Reaching the end of the alley, I turn left again, which takes me out onto the main road. I look back down to the shop and see thick, black smoke and flames licking at the side of the building, but the weirdest thing are the bodies on fire just standing there, like they haven't got the sense or intelligence to move away. Even the ones standing on the outside aren't moving away. They just stand and wait, and then catch alight.

I move away and head towards the garage, thinking about how they seem to follow each other. Last night, I watched as they massed at the front of my house and behind my front door. But I was screaming abuse at them from my window, alerting them to my presence. Then the armoured van went past, sounding the horn repeatedly. Was it the noise of the horn that pulled them away or the already huge stream of other infected in its wake?

The thoughts give me hope. Maybe I can carry something that will distract them with movement or noise – something I can throw if I get cornered or trapped. There are plenty of children's toys that bounce about with loud noises and flashing lights. I should have kept a can of lighter fluid and matches... I could set one of them on fire, which will draw others to it while I get away. The thought process makes me realise how much I need supplies and weapons. The bat is good. It's longer than the hammer and means I can keep them away from me. A gun would be perfect, but I have no idea where to find one. The only guns in Britain are shotguns and farmer rifles. Even a double-barrelled shotgun only gives two shots at a time, but a shotgun is also long and heavy – like a bat.

I think of the movies and news reports of robbers using sawed-off shotguns. That would make them smaller and lighter to carry but reduces their secondary use as a blunt instrument or a ranged weapon.

The police have guns. You see them quite a lot these days – armed police, with pistols on their belts. They keep the bigger guns locked in armoured boxes in their cars. I guess there must be armouries in the police stations.

That gives me another thought... Maybe the police are holed up in their stations? If they have weapons and strong buildings, they could remain safely inside. Boroughfare has a police station in the town centre; maybe I should have gone there first.

Ridiculously, I wonder if they would arrest me if I was armed with a gun.

CHAPTER SIX

Finally, I reach the sprawling collection of buildings, workshops, and lockups at the end of the village.

Big double wooden doors face out onto a hardstand. Oil stains on the ground, and a single fuel pump in the middle, hardly used as the price is always so much cheaper at the supermarkets.

There are, however, two cars parked up. One on a jack, with the driver's side wheel missing, and the other one a tiny, silver Nissan Micra, which, unfortunately, is locked.

I head over to the reception door, which is also locked, and look through the window to see the lights are off and no obvious sign of movement from within. There might be an easier way in at the back, so I trot off, looking for another door while hoping the Micra is just in for a service and isn't broken down or something.

More doors at the back, but they're all strong looking, and the few windows are barred too. Back at the front, I check the double doors, but they are flush together and well secured. The reception door is the best option as the top half is a large glass pane.

I stand listening for a few seconds, knowing I'll have to be quick: smash the glass, get in, find the keys, get out, and go.

I pull the bat back and swing at the glass pane in the door. The glass is toughened and fractures, but stays in place. Another swing, and the bat smashes a hole in the glass, but the pane remains in place. It takes bloody ages and makes a hell of a noise too. I should have bust a door open or, you know, like shouted that I am here to alert every single infected person in a ten-mile radius.

Eventually, and after much sweating, kicking, cursing, some sulking, and some more swearing, I finally bust a hole big enough to climb through.

I slip my bag off and put it through the hole, then climb in, which is harder than I thought it would be as the bottom ledge is too high to step over, and I don't want to enter head-first, so I hop my right leg in and straddle the bottom of the frame, then shift my weight over to draw my remaining leg in. Which is all going swimmingly until the bloody burglar alarm goes off. Screeching merrily away after sneakily waiting for me to smash a massive hole in the door.

'Bastard fucking shitty, cunty, bastard arsing, cock-faced fucking thing!' I fall inside, grab my bat, and smash the alarm box off the wall, which warbles sadly before cutting out. 'Wanker,' I mutter, giving it what for before heading deeper into the place, seeing a counter for fuel payment and stuff for sale. Oils and lubricants, and other stuff. No keys, though. Why would there be keys? It's not like anything is trying to be helpful right now, is it?

I go behind the counter and check drawers and cupboards – again, nothing.

A door leads into the workshop area, and I go through. It's very dark as the grimy windows are not letting much light in, so I flick the lights on and wait for the fluorescent strips to blink on.

Tool drawers and various machinery are positioned around the outside, with shiny, red sets of sliding metal trays, with cool logos on them – everything seems to have a *Snap-on* sticker on it, but there is a small metal key cupboard on the wall. Which is locked. Awesome.

I search and find a large, flat-headed screwdriver. Taking this back, I force the end into the gap between the metal door and the frame, levering hard to prise the door open.

Inside are a few rows of hooks, with various keys hanging down and two sets of car keys on fobs. One of them has the *Nissan* logo on a metal clasp. I take the keys and head back into reception to see an infected woman trying to walk forward while leaning her head and shoulders through the hole in the door.

I use the bat and strike downwards on her head. The impact bends her over the frame, and I swing upwards, smashing her back out of the door, and I gingerly peek out to see her stretched out and motionless, with her head at an unnatural angle. The neck broken from either the force of the blow or the impact from hitting the ground.

I start to clamber through, but my rucksack gets caught, so I go back in and take the rucksack off, throw it out, and try again, tripping as I go and nearly landing face first on the dead woman. I roll off with a yelp, grab my bag and bat, and rush to the car before anything else happens.

At least I got the right keys and gain entry to the Micra without anything exploding or making noise. And while looking about, I turn the key in the ignition and shoot forward with a jolt.

'FUCK,' I scream out in frustration at my own rushed,

panicked state and try again, but this time, I keep my foot down on the clutch and make sure the manual gearstick is in neutral.

The car starts, and I pull away from the village, glancing repeatedly at the rearview mirror and the plumes of black smoke billowing up into the sky.

The fire will spread quickly in the warm, dry weather, and I think of all the damage being caused. No fire engines will come racing to the rescue. No police will cordon off the area, and no ambulances will ever arrive to treat the wounded and hurt.

It will just burn and burn until there is nothing left.

CHAPTER SEVEN

**'There are survivors. You are not alone.
Do not come to London. We are completely
infested.
I repeat, DO NOT COME TO LONDON.
If you are in the south, then we advise you head
to the Victorian Forts on the south coast.
Take whatever supplies you can carry: water,
food, medicine, and clothing.
Stay out of the cities and towns. Head to the
forts on the coast.'**

A deep, reassuring voice blasting from the radio on a loop that repeats over and over, with a faint click between each repeat. I found it by turning the radio on and twisting the old-style manual tuning dial until the voice was coming from the speakers, making my heart race again.

I keep listening to it, hoping someone alive will cut in and speak, but it just repeats over and over.

It's still calming, though, and whoever recorded it did so without hint of panic of distress. I try to picture the man recording the message, and my mind creates an image of an older, refined man, groomed and sophisticated, with a beard, definitely a beard.

I think of the forts on the south known as Palmerston's Follies and what I remember from school history lessons. I know they were built during the 1800s to fight off a French invasion that never happened. There's quite a few of them, I think, dotted along the coast.

Some of them have fallen to ruin, but then I'm sure a few have been preserved by historical societies, and I curse myself for not paying more attention to my own local history.

The most famous are the three or four big, round things in The Solent, the stretch of water that separates the mainland from the Isle of Wight. They are amazing feats of engineering, used now as private hotels or left to decay.

If I can get to my parents, I could send them to the forts and then try to find my sister.

The message on the radio says London is infested and not to go there, but I'm not leaving her. If there is a chance that she is holed up at home, then I have to try.

☙ ❧

THE REST of the drive is, thankfully, uneventful, and I soon reach my parents' small village and slow down on seeing a gathering of people outside their local shop, wincing when I realise they're just more infected, and I tense up, praying that I don't see my dad amongst them. He always goes down for the early paper and could have walked unwittingly into them without realising what was happening.

He's not there, and I let the breath go, offering a quick prayer to any God listening.

Unlike the previous village, this shop is on the main through-road, and it's a modern, large convenience store, more like a mini supermarket, and as I go past, I see movement inside. I think to keep going, then slow down, and realise my dad might be inside. What if he went for his newspaper and managed to run and hide like I did? Maybe I should go home and check first, but if he is inside, I could be too late if I have to come back, and I'd never forgive myself for that.

I slow the car and look back at the infected people. Five of them, three males and two females.

One of them looks like a delivery driver, wearing matching blue trousers and jacket. Another is very old. Even from here, I can see his hunched-over, thin frame and wispy, grey hair, with a white vest tucked into his sleeping shorts pulled up nearly to his chest.

The two women are late middle-aged, and both dressed in sensible trousers and sleeveless jackets with pastel-coloured shirts. They look like the early-to-bed and early-to-rise types, who only drink sherry at the weekends, and who are always perfectly behaved and have expertly trained, small dogs. Fortunately, there's no zombie dogs that I can see anywhere. Can dogs even get infected? I have no idea. The last one is a young male, dressed in jeans and a t-shirt.

I watch them all shuffling outside the shop, pressing their bodies against the door and windows. I can't see any more of them anywhere. Just these five. Shit. I just want to go, but I can't risk my dad being inside.

Right. Decision made, but if I'm going to do this, then I

have to be quick. The noise and movement might draw more, and I don't want to end up trapped inside too.

I ease out and leave the engine running for a quick getaway, and take my bat as I head towards the infected. Then I stop and go back to close the car door, with the image of an infected person getting in and waiting for me on the backseat.

Too many movies.

I slam the door on purpose so they hear me and watch as the old man turns around to start shuffling towards me straight away; then within seconds, they're all moving towards me, as though an unspoken message has passed between them.

I need to separate them as they are too close together for me to risk attacking them all in one go. Even with the range of the baseball bat, it would only take one of them to lunge quickly, and I could get bitten.

I look at the area, noting the pavement has obstacles: a bike rack, litter bins, and a post box. There is a high step down from the pavement to the road. These are things which will impede my movements and could cause me to trip or fall, but the road is wide and clear, with no obstructions.

Moving off to my right, I lure them into clear ground. I'm choosing my battleground, selecting where to fight, and it feels strange. There is almost a sense of excitement, a weird feeling, like just before the roller coaster moves off. I am scared yet exhilarated.

The old man is nearest. He saw me first and has the head start. I thought his old age would make him slower, and the others would go past him, but they move at roughly the same speed. It appears the infected are not hampered by age or infirmity.

Watching the old man come towards me makes me uneasy – he looks very old and frail, and I'm getting the same feeling as I had when the girl in the blue dress was in front of me. Attacking a woman or the elderly seems wrong. Then I remember how I felt after the motorway when that woman tried to bite me and suffocate me with her boobs.

They're not people. They are infected.

I raise the bat up, poised and ready, and wait for him to come, watching the saliva hanging down from his mouth, and he pulls his lips back as I snort a dry laugh at the sight of his gummy, toothless mouth. What's he going to do? Suck on me?

He should be carrying a blender or a knife and fork or maybe have a carer to help him make flesh soup. I almost feel sorry for him, and then I see his hands curled up like claws with nasty, jagged fingernails and remember the strength of the woman from the car accident was incredible, and he probably has the same strength too. His fingernails look like they could rip flesh open.

Fuck him. I step forward and swing the bat hard into the side of his head, and he goes spinning off to my left.

I move to the right, going around the side of the small group as they all turn to follow me. I move back to the left, and they all turn again. I move right, and again, they all move as one. Synchronised zombies.

I lead them into the road before I run round the back of them, watching as they do a shuffling about turn and bump into each other; then I see my advantage and dart forward to whack the delivery driver hard on the shoulder, sending him into the two women, knocking them away and creating more space between them all.

The delivery driver goes down with one of the women. Both of them groaning audibly as they start trying to get back up but hamper their own efforts by constantly pushing each other back down. The old man is still down, and the young lad is closest now.

I step out so that I'm facing his left side and smash the bat into his face. His nose explodes, with a sickening crunch of bones that I hear upon the impact of the bat. He stumbles backwards and falls onto his arse, but instantly tries to get back up, so I bunch power and strike the side of his head like a golf-swing and send him flying off to the side.

A growl behind, and I spin round just as the other dog walker woman lunges at me, with her lips pulled back, showing her teeth. I aim an uppercut but miss, and stagger forward into her with the momentum of the swing. A mistake made, and quick as a flash, she's into me, driving forward as I try and go back, and trip over one of the others I knocked down. Sprawling out on the ground, and suddenly, this seems like a very bad idea very poorly executed.

Growls and groans all around me as I lash out with the bat, whacking bodies, but they keep coming in. The old man crawling at my side. I whack him hard with the bat, then roll the other way into the other woman, who tries to lunge in for the bite, and in the panic, I just about get the end of the bat into the side of her head, pushing her away as the other woman staggers in and readies to drop on me. I get a foot up into her belly, holding her off while she dangles down, drooling spit down my leg while I whack small, hard hits into the other one.

'SHIT!' I cry out as the delivery driver comes in from the other side and take a quick swing to keep him away. On my back, with one leg up, holding the woman at bay while hitting left and right, twisting from the torso while my stomach muscles scream in pain, and then, if that wasn't enough, old, gummy grandad joins in and starts crawling back. 'FUCK IT!' A nice, healthy dose of fresh rage detonates, and I start lashing out with hard, brutal hits before wrenching to the side and letting the woman braced against my leg fall down next to me, giving me space to get up and away. But no. That can't happen because the young man, who should be bloody dead, is back on his sodding feet and coming in to join the feast. Wank it, and at the point, I think I am royally screwed, but a young Asian lad appears behind the young man and swings a cricket bat into his head, driving him away.

'Thank fuck!' On my feet, and I start laying about me with the bat, hitting heads and body parts while the Asian boy does the same. Both of us bashing skulls until I stagger back, gasping for air and looking at the mangled corpses littering the ground while the lad carries on, battering down at one of the women, hitting her over and over.

'I think she's finished, mate,' I say as he carries on. 'Mate, she's definitely finished. Or, you know, just carry on...' I add as he unleashes a fresh barrage of blows.

Eventually, he stops and steps backwards, holding the bat with both hands down at his front. Blood all over his shiny, white trainers. He looks young, no more than fifteen years old, dark-skinned with black, gelled hair. Indian or Pakistani, maybe Sri Lankan, but his eyes are blazing from the kill.

Behind him, the shop door opens, and an older woman comes running out, angrily yelling at the boy. 'What did you do that for? I told you to stay inside.'

The boy spins, seeing his mother coming, and swallows while darting a look at me.

'He was trying to help us,' the boy shouts back, squeaky and high-pitched, showing his age.

'No, *you* could have been killed, you foolish boy, and

don't talk back to me! Don't you *ever* talk back to me!' she shouts back at him with a mother's fear-loaded anger and switches into a language I can't understand until he finally hangs his head with a look of shame and starts back towards the shop. The woman stays and looks at me, and when she speaks, her tone is forcefully polite.

'Thank you for what you did. I am sorry for my son; he is young and foolish...' she trails off, looking about at the bodies and the woman's brains beaten out of her head. 'I can't believe what's happened...what's happening, this is... just so... Have you seen more of them? We tried calling the police, but we cannot get through – 999 is not working. We cannot get hold of anyone.'

'It's everywhere,' I reply, wiping the sweat from my face as the adrenalin once more wears off. 'I'm from Borough-fare, and the whole town is gone. I went through Littleton on the way here; that's gone too... I, er, I saw it on the news last night. I think it's worldwide...' I take my turn to trail off as the blood drains from her face, and she presses a hand to her cheek.

'I'm, er, looking for my dad, Howard. He comes down every morning for a newspaper. Have you seen him?'

She stays silent for a few seconds.

'I'm sorry, what...what did you say?' She looks back at me with a confused expression.

'My dad...Howard? He comes down every morning for a newspaper. Have you seen him today?'

'Oh, Howard. Yes, we know Howard, always so polite. No, we have not seen him. There is just my family – my son and daughter, and me, of course.'

'Is your husband not with you?'

'No, he is visiting family at home in India...' her voice becomes very soft.

'I'm sure he is okay. Maybe it is just Europe that's affected. Look, why don't you go inside? It's not safe out here in the open.'

'Yes... Do you want to come in?'

'No, thank you. I have to go to my parents' house; they live on the estate. Listen, I heard a broadcast on the radio, and it said that people should go to the forts.'

'What forts?'

'The old ones, the Palmerston Forts. There's quite a few of them all along the coast. The radio said London was infested, and people should head over to the forts and take food, water, and medicine.'

'Oh, I think we should stay here and wait for help. We have enough food, thank you.'

'I don't think it will be safe here; those *things* are everywhere,' I point at the bodies on the ground. 'And other people might want to take your food. Maybe you should take what you can carry and go. Do you have a vehicle?'

'We have a van – my husband uses it for the cash-and-carry.'

'Take your van, load it up with as much as you can take, and then leave,' I urge her.

'What about my husband? What if he comes back and cannot find us?'

'Leave a note for him, and also one that tells other people where you have gone so they can go there too, but do it quickly.' She glances back at the shop, clearly unsure of what to do. I can see her dilemma – the shop looks strong and secure, a safe place. 'I saw these things last night. They were different. They weren't slow like these were. They were fast. If they change again, they won't stop until they have got you and your family.'

She stares back at me. The suggestion of a threat to her family has sharpened her instincts for survival.

'Where are these forts?'

'Check the Internet if it's still working. If not, look at local maps. Do you sell maps?'

'Yes...yes, we have maps.'

'Check them and find the nearest fort, then load up, and go. Please don't stay here. It's not safe.'

She goes to move away, then hesitates. 'Will you come? We could travel together...'

'I can't. I'm sorry... I have to find my family. I'll try and get my parents to follow you. I'll ask them to come here first and see if you are still here, but don't wait for them, load up, and get going.'

She nods and walks back to the shop, still in shock. I'm worried that she's not taken it in and will try to wait it out. Her son comes out of the door, walking towards his mother. A teenage girl comes out behind him and stands back, holding the door open.

'Hey, thanks for your help again, mate. I just said to your mother that people are going to the forts on the coast. She said you had a van. I really think you should load up with food and water and go there as soon as possible. Take anything you can carry.'

'Are you going there too?'

His mother interrupts before I can answer, 'No, he has to find his family. Go back inside, please.'

I turn and walk to the car, and head into the estate. My parents moved here a few years ago. The old house was the family home. This is their new house, and it feels different, still homely and welcoming, but not the same.

My dad retired two years ago. He was an engineer for a telecoms company and had a good retirement package, but he quickly got bored of playing golf and went back as a part-timer.

My sister and I bought him a new set of clubs for his 60th birthday. Well, I say *we* bought them, but my sister paid most of it as she earns a fortune. I paid what I could, but still, it's the thought that counts.

Their new house is detached and modern, but the large driveway is empty. Dad bought a new Toyota when he retired and always leaves it on the driveway, proudly cleaning it at every opportunity.

I leave the Micra on the street, with the keys in the ignition, and walk towards the house, seeing the front door and all the windows are closed.

The first bad sign is that the front door has been left unlocked, and I enter, with my bat gripped and ready, pausing for a minute in the hallway, eyeing the stairs ahead of me. The lounge to the left. The dining room to my right. Silence inside, and I close the front door gently behind me.

I want to call out but don't want to risk alerting any infected that I am here. I go into the lounge and then the dining room, and finally the kitchen to see two half-drunk mugs of coffee on the side; both are cold.

I go upstairs, with my bat raised, but find nothing in the two guest rooms. The bathroom is clear.

My parents' bedroom is also vacant. The drawers are empty and thrown around, and the wardrobe is open, with clothes lying about. It looks like they were in a rush. I go back downstairs and check the rooms again, finally spotting the notepad on the dining room table, with a handwritten note in my mother's writing.

HOWIE,

Dad got a phone call last night from an old colleague working in France. They said what was happening, awful things. Dad spoke to your sister. Sarah is safe at home, locked in and secure. The phone line went down when we were talking to her. We kept trying to call you, but all the numbers were engaged. We are going to come and get you, but I suppose if you are reading this, then we have missed each other.

Stay here, Howie. We will try your place and come back here before we get Sarah. We left the front door unlocked in case you left your key behind. You can lock the door, though. We both have our keys.

Please stay here, Howie. We will be back soon.

Love, Mum and Dad.

I READ the note over a few times. Sarah is safe, thank God. The relief is massive and washes over me, with a great sense of fatigue following close behind. Hunger too. I head into the kitchen and find a Cornish pasty in the fridge that I wolf down in seconds, followed by another, then a mug of hot, sweet tea.

I try the home phone but find it dead – there is not even a dial tone. I check the router. Lights flashing red – no Internet and no phone line.

After locking the front door, I go upstairs into the bath-room, strip off, and have a hot shower, watching as the water runs red and black from the gore and grime while wondering how long it will be before the power goes off.

My clothes are too dirty to put back on. They're covered

in blood and need to be thrown away. The blood could be infectious, but then I would have nothing to wear.

I remember that there are some old clothes of mine in bin liners in the loft. I'd left them at the old house, and Mum kept nagging me to go and sort them out, which I never did.

I wrap a towel around my waist and find the long stick to open the loft hatch, and climb into the loft, and turn the light on. The loft is boarded out, and I can see a pile of black bags with white, sticky labels marked 'Howie'.

I find an old pair of jeans I used to live in years ago, then a white t-shirt to go with it until I stop and think that maybe white will stand out a bit. Plus, it shows the dirt and gore a bit too well. I put it back and find an old, black jumper instead.

Finally, with nothing left to do but wait, I go into the lounge and lay down on the sofa, thinking through all that has happened. Thinking of the horror and carnage. Of the death and awful things I have seen, and for a second, my mind buzzes with emotions and weird feelings, and I think I'll never be able to sleep again.

But then within seconds, my eyes grow heavy, and my breathing slows, and eventually, after jerking awake a couple of times, I drift off to sleep.

ALSO BY RR HAYWOOD

Washington Post, Wall Street Journal, Audible & Amazon Allstar bestselling author, RR Haywood. One of the top ten most downloaded indie authors in the UK with over four million books sold and nearly 40 Kindle bestsellers.

GASLIT

The Instant #1 Amazon Bestseller.

A Twisted Tale Of Manipulation & Murder.

Audio Narrated by Gethin Anthony

A dark, noir, psychological thriller with rave reviews across multiple countries.

A new job awaits. **Huntington House** *needs a live-in security guard to prevent access during an inheritance dispute.*

This is exactly what Mike needs: a new start in a new place and a chance to turn things around.

It all seems perfect, especially when he meets Tessa.

But **Huntington House holds dark secrets**. *Bumps in the night. Flickering lights. Music playing from somewhere.*

Mike's mind starts to unravel as he questions his sanity in the dark, claustrophobic corridors and rooms.

Something isn't right.

There is someone else in the house.

The pressure grows as the people around Mike get pulled into a web of lies and manipulation, forcing him to take action before it's too late.

-

DELIO. PHASE ONE

*WINNER OF "*BEST NEW BOOK*" DISCOVER SCI-FI 2023

#1 Amazon & Audible bestseller

A single bed in a small room.

The centre of Piccadilly Circus.

A street in New York city outside of a 7-Eleven.

A young woman taken from her country.

A drug dealer who paid his debt.

A suicidal, washed-up cop.

The rest of the world now frozen.

Unmoving.

Unblinking.

"Brilliant."

"A gripping story. Harrowing, and often hysterical."

"This book is very different to anything else out there - and brilliantly so."

"You'll fall so hard for these characters, you'll wish the world would freeze just so you could stay with them forever."

*

FICTION LAND

*Nominated for Best Audio Book at the British Book Awards 2023

Not many men get to start over.

John Croker did and left his old life behind – until crooks stole his delivery van. No van means no pay, which means his niece doesn't get the life-saving operation she needs, and so in desperation, John uses the skills of his former life one last time... That is until he dies and wakes up in Fiction Land. A city occupied by characters from unfinished novels.

But the world around him doesn't feel right, and when he starts asking questions, the authorities soon take extreme measures to stop him finding the truth about Fiction Land.

*

EXTRACTED SERIES

EXTRACTED

EXECUTED

EXTINCT

Blockbuster Time-Travel

#1 Amazon US

#1 Amazon UK

#1 Audible US & UK

Washington Post & Wall Street Journal Bestseller

In 2061, a young scientist invents a time machine to fix a tragedy in his past. But his good intentions turn catastrophic when an early test reveals something unexpected: the end of the world.

A desperate plan is formed. Recruit three heroes, ordinary humans capable of extraordinary things, and change the future.

Safa Patel is an elite police officer, on duty when Downing Street comes under terrorist attack. As armed men storm through the breach, she dispatches them all.

'Mad' Harry Madden is a legend of the Second World War. Not only did he complete an impossible mission—to plant charges on a heavily defended submarine base—but he also escaped with his life.

Ben Ryder is just an insurance investigator. But as a young man he witnessed a gang assaulting a woman and her child. He went to their rescue, and killed all five.

Can these three heroes, extracted from their timelines at the point of death, save the world?

*

THE CODE SERIES

The Worldship Humility

The Elfor Drop

The Elfor One

#1 Audible bestselling smash hit narrated by Colin Morgan

#1 Amazon bestselling Science-Fiction

"A rollicking, action packed space adventure…"

Sam, an airlock operative, is bored. Living in space should be full of adventure, except it isn't, and he fills his time hacking 3-D movie posters.

Petty thief Yasmine Dufont grew up in the lawless lower levels of the ship, surrounded by violence and squalor, and now she wants out. She wants to escape to the luxury of the Ab-Spa, where they eat real food instead of rats and synth cubes.

Meanwhile, the sleek-hulled, unmanned Gagarin has come back from the ever-continuing search for a new home. Nearly all hope is lost that a new planet will ever be found, until the Gagarin returns with a code of information that suggests a habitable planet has been found. This news should be shared with the whole fleet, but a few rogue captains want to colonise it for themselves.

When Yasmine inadvertently steals the code, she and Sam become caught up in a dangerous game of murder, corruption, political wrangling and...porridge, with sex-addicted Detective Zhang Woo hot on their heels, his own life at risk if he fails to get the code back.

*

THE UNDEAD SERIES

THE UK's #1 Horror Series

Available on Amazon & Audible

"The Best Series Ever..."

The Undead. The First Seven Days

The Undead. The Second Week.

The Undead Day Fifteen.

The Undead Day Sixteen.

The Undead Day Seventeen

The Undead Day Eighteen

The Undead Day Nineteen

The Undead Day Twenty

The Undead Day Twenty-One

The Undead Twenty-Two

The Undead Twenty-Three: The Fort

The Undead Twenty-Four: Equilibrium

The Undead Twenty-Five: The Heat

The Undead Twenty-Six: Rye

The Undead Twenty-Seven: The Garden Centre

The Undead Twenty-Eight: Return To The Fort

The Undead Twenty-Nine: Hindhead Part 1

The Undead Thirty: Hindhead Part 2

The Undead Thirty-One: Winchester

The Undead Thirty-Two: The Battle For Winchester

The Undead Thirty-Three: The One True Race

Blood on the Floor

An Undead novel

Blood at the Premiere

An Undead novel

The Camping Shop

An Undead novella

*

A Town Called Discovery

The #1 Amazon & Audible Time Travel Thriller

A man falls from the sky. He has no memory.

What lies ahead are a series of tests. Each more brutal than the last, and if he gets through them all, he might just reach A Town Called Discovery.

*

THE FOUR WORLDS OF BERTIE CAVENDISH

A rip-roaring multiverse time-travel crossover starring:

The Undead

Extracted.

A Town Called Discovery

and featuring

The Worldship Humility

*

www.rrhaywood.com

Find me on Facebook:
https://www.facebook.com/RRHaywood/

Find me on TikTok (The Writing Class for the Working Class)
https://www.tiktok.com/@rr.haywood

Find me on X:
https://twitter.com/RRHaywood

Printed in Great Britain
by Amazon

51409119R00050